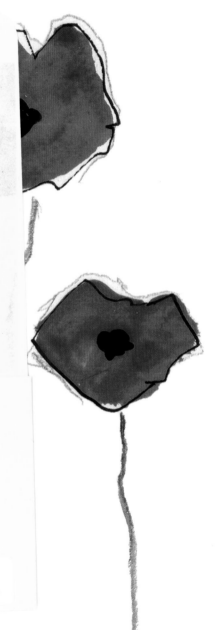

Text and illustrations © 2018 Jacques Goldstyn
Originally published under the title *Jules et Jim: frères d'armes* in 2018
   by Bayard Canada Livres inc.
Translated by Anne Louise Mahoney. Translation © Owlkids Books, 2018.
Published by permission of Bayard Canada Livres inc., Montréal, QC.

Owlkids Books acknowledges the financial support of the Canada Council for the Arts, the
Ontario Arts Council, the Government of Canada through the Canada Book Fund (CBF) and
the Government of Ontario through the Ontario Media Development Corporation's Book
Initiative for our publishing activities.

Published in Canada by
Owlkids Books Inc.
1 Eglinton Avenue East
Toronto, ON M4P 3A1

Published in the United States by
Owlkids Books Inc.
1700 Fourth Street
Berkeley, CA 94710

Library and Archives Canada Cataloguing in Publication

Goldstyn, Jacques
[Jules et Jim. English]
      The eleventh hour / Jacques Goldstyn.

Translation of: Jules et Jim, frères d'armes.
Translated by Anne Louise Mahoney.
ISBN 978-1-77147-348-4 (hardcover)

      I. Title. II. Title: Jules et Jim. English

PS8613.O448J8413 2018   jC843'.6   C2018-901128-9

Library of Congress Control Number: 2018934227

Manufactured in Dongguan, China, in November 2018, by Toppan Leefung Packaging &
Printing (Dongguan) Co., Ltd.
Job #BAYDC56/R1

B   C   D   E   F   G

Publisher of Chirp, Chickadee and OWL
www.owlkidsbooks.com

| Owlkids Books is a division of **Bayard** CANADA

The Eleventh Hour

Jacques Goldstyn

OWLKIDS BOOKS

Jules and Jim were born on the same day,
in the same town.

Jim was born first.
Jules arrived two minutes later.

Jules and Jim soon became best friends.

They liked the same things and
they played the same games.

But Jim always took the lead.
He was faster and stronger than Jules.

Jules looked up to Jim, and Jim looked out for Jules.

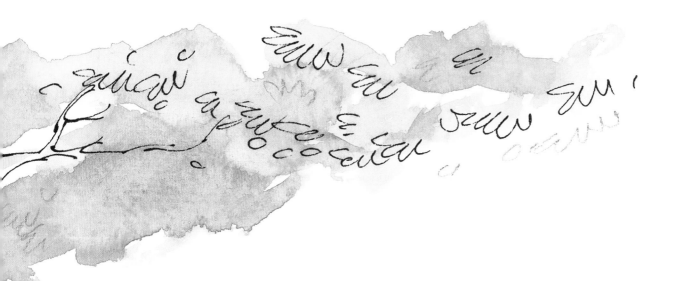

Everyone agreed: Jules and Jim were an odd pair.

Years passed and nothing changed.

Jules was always two minutes behind Jim, which caused him a lot of trouble.

Everyone laughed at Jules … except Jim.

Life could have kept going like this,

but one day, a war began across the ocean, somewhere in Europe …

... because an archduke and his wife were assassinated.

Europe divided into two enemy camps.

And Canada was at war with Germany.

Jules and Jim didn't understand all the news reports about treaties and alliances, but they understood that their country needed them.

So the two friends enlisted in the army. They had to beat those German monsters.

Jim was first in line for his pack.

His uniform fit like a glove.

Jules arrived two minutes too late.

He got the leftovers.

Jules and Jim had to go through rigorous training.

Jules quickly learned that orders were meant to be obeyed.

Then, after months of training …

. . . they left for Europe.

Jules showed up two minutes late.

When they finally arrived in France after more training in England, the Canadian soldiers received a jubilant welcome.

They left for the front lines right away.

Jules and Jim had imagined war to be full
of epic battles and glorious charges.

They were surprised to find muddy trenches
surrounded by barbed wire instead.

LONDON
385 miles

They saw action almost immediately. Huge shells fell like rain for hours.

Then, after a lull, the Germans attacked on foot.

But the Canadian soldiers pushed them back with machine guns.

Then the Canadians began shelling the Germans.

Before long, it was time for the Canadian attack.

The soldiers knew running toward the enemy trenches was madness, but they had to follow orders.

The attacks often ended in failure, and the soldiers who were
still alive stumbled back to their trenches.

They would hide there until the next attack. And then
it would start all over again.

Over the top and back ... Over the top and back ...

Life in the trenches was difficult,
except for a few rare moments.

The soldiers always had wet feet, they were covered
with lice, and the trenches were full of rats.

Jules became very good at catching them.

The soldiers started to look like cavemen.

Sometimes they took German prisoners and, to Jules and Jim's surprise, they didn't seem like monsters. They were kind of pitiful.

Deep down, Jules and Jim envied the prisoners a bit, because for them, the war was over.

But for the two friends, the slaughter continued with weapons
that were more and more terrible:
fighter planes, poison gas, tanks …

The war was like a huge cauldron that kept devouring men.

As the war dragged on, life away from the front lines became more and more difficult.

Women had replaced men in many jobs . . .

... including at munitions factories, which were open around the clock.

Handling the explosives turned their skin yellow.

At the front, Jim was always the first to attack.

Jules always followed two minutes behind.

Which was why Jim was decorated,

while Jules got stuck doing chores.

But in spite of his medals, Jim was afraid, too.

Sometimes at night, the two friends hugged each other.

Sometimes they even cried as they talked about going home.

Montreal
5297mi

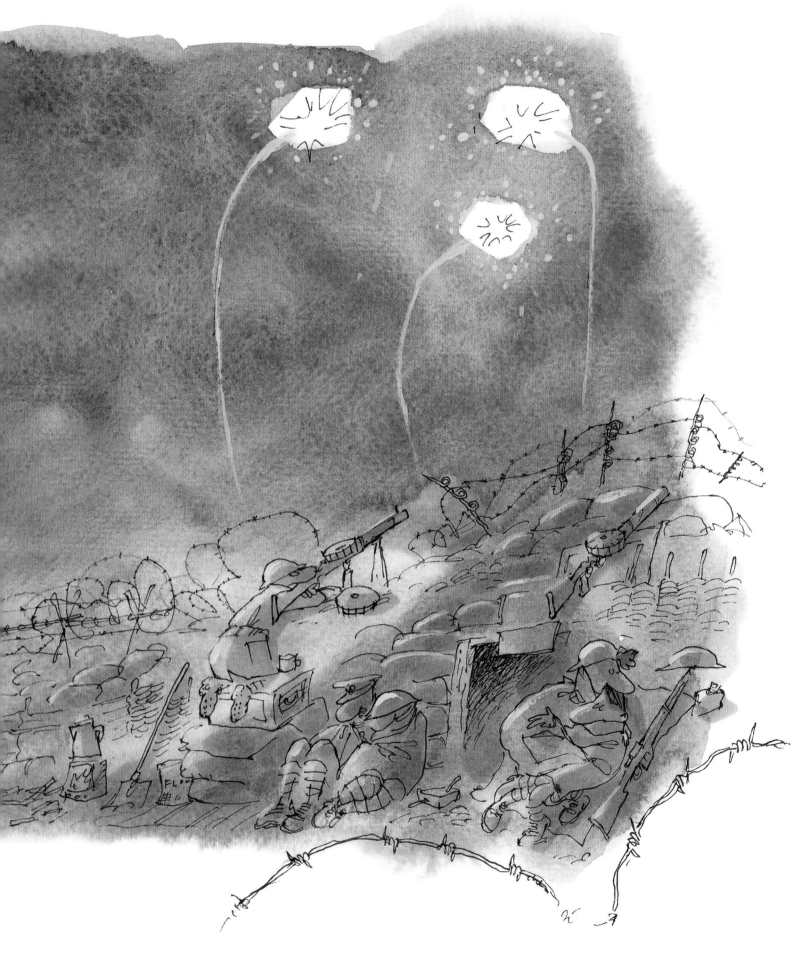

The war lasted a long time.

Soldiers on both sides were exhausted.

And back in Germany, hungry citizens
were protesting against the war.

Germany decided to stop fighting.

On November 11, 1918, at five o'clock in the morning, the leaders of the Allies met the German leaders in a clearing near the front,

where they signed the armistice.

The fighting was supposed to stop right away, but they decided to wait until eleven o'clock to start the cease-fire, to give time for word to spread to the troops.

That meant the fighting would end at the eleventh hour of the eleventh day of the eleventh month.

But meanwhile, on the battlefields, even though the armistice had been signed hours earlier, the fighting continued as if nothing had changed.

Shortly before the cease-fire was set to begin, Jim and Jules were ordered to attack.

As always, Jim went over the top first. Jules followed just in time to see Jim shot.

It was 10:58, two minutes before the war ended.

Jules did everything he could to save Jim,
but his friend died in his arms.

It was the end of the war . . .

. . . and it was the end for Jim.

Jules came home without his friend.

He found it hard to live a normal life again.

He couldn't stop thinking about Jim.

Returning to civilian life was not easy.

Jules tried all kinds of different jobs …

In the end, he became a watchmaker.

Jules' watches had one odd thing in common: they all ran two minutes slow.

In memory of George Lawrence Price, the last Canadian
soldier to die on November 11, 1918. He was killed at 10:58 a.m.,
two minutes before the armistice ended the First World War.

I dedicate this book to my grandfather, Michel Quélé'ver, a Breton farmer who loved life and animals.
He often said he'd been through the "entire war of 14-18," which is how the First World War is often referred to in France.
One day, when my mother was eight years old, she asked her father how many Germans he had killed. My grandfather, who was normally a gentle man, replied sternly:
"Never ask me this question again."
He knew he was lucky to have escaped the war uninjured.
However, some injuries are invisible.
I would like to have known my grandfather.
I would have asked him so many questions.

Jacques Goldstyn